CW00382370

JoJo's Amazing Adventure

and other short stories

---

by John Robinson

I dedicate this book to my parents

A CIP catalogue record for this title may be available from the British Library

Contents

1 : Introduction

This is my first book. And by that count, it is very dear to my heart. It took me many years of reading and rewriting short stories, taken from the Chinese, Indian and Arabian peninsulas to finally come up with something that I am happy with. But I haven't plagiarized them. I literally rewrote a selection of them, and then lost the file, so I had to do it again and again.

JoJo the protagonist makes a fleeting appearance, but the depth and scope of this novel extends far out from just one little man, onto the world at large. A world of our dreams, sometimes manifest, and at other's hidden. This is his story, and it is God's, and now it is yours. Enjoy!

2 : The Beginning

JoJo lay outstretched on a beach. The sea gently lapping his heels. He moved out his arm and clenched his hand into a fist. It responded to touch, but only barely. He had no memory. He could not remember who he was or how he had gotten there. He didn't remember lying parched in the baking sun dehydrating and burning like a cat on fire, half an hour ago. Or half an hour before that, how he had clung to a piece of driftwood through the gentle ocean currents which had irrevocably placed him there.

Much less half an hour before that when desperate and panic-stricken his body had involuntarily convulsed in a series of spasms as their transport touched zero. Or half an hour before that when their pilot announced they 'might have a problem'. All he remembered was an insatiable thirst, and a need to feel wanted.

Trying to shake himself out of the miserable pit which he seemed to be digging for himself, the man without a name pressed hard against the sand and slowly lifted himself up. As his eyes refocused in the bright light, he could make out trees and shrubs ahead, which he made his way towards.

Once out of the blazing heat, he tried to recollect some more. He could ascertain from the smart rags he was wearing, shirt and black trousers, that he was some kind of businessman apparently on a mission. But to what purpose the extent of his endeavor was, escaped him. He thought he might be bi-lingual, although if you asked him to count to ten in English at that precise point he would struggle. He was not particularly muscular or athletic. Or immediately filled with a profound knowledge of electrical engineering, bricklaying, or anything like that.

Yet he was still convinced, even definitely now, that his was a mission of vital importance, not only for his own wellbeing but also perhaps, for that of the survival of the whole planet. Much less did he realize in his half delirious and stricken state, that he might just be right.

I want to paint you a picture of a world where champion knights ride off with their princesses, sparkling gardens bloom with different colored flowers every day of the year, and chivalrous wanderers give up life and limb to rescue the innocent and harmless public.

A world where kind and brave kings are consoled by old wise wizards to govern over plentiful and healthy lands populated by hardworking and bountiful citizens. A world where blacksmiths sweat in the heat of their furnaces to weld majestic harnesses to ride great white Arabian horses.

These themselves being ridden by excellent knights and jockeys. Where the music is always good and the beer always flowing. Where lovers never grumble, and children never cry. In fact, in this world everyone is a vegetarian, and by that, I mean that they don't eat meat. Only organic vegetables and occasionally fish but even that not very often.

Which doesn't matter because all people, both sexes, were good cooks, and they create tasty and scrumptious meals across the weeks. Even their horses were happy being fed green grasses supplemented with the occasional orange carrot or red apple. So, the world was at one.

Jackie was a dreamer. She had a gorgeous silk blue bed with velvet crimson cushions and pitch-black shutters. She didn't do anything, just lay on her bed, and slept. But my what dreams! She dreamt of leaving her little abode and flying off to far away shores from whence she would meet and defeat a whole manner of demons and dragons, before safely returning to her little home to finish her night's sleep.

She dreamt of a world where children always thanked their parents for Christmas and their parents always thanked Santa for them. Where Rudolf's nose was always bright red and poems always rhymed and rhythmed.

But unfortunately, sure as night follows day and cough follows cold, Jackie's dreams were always interrupted by something. Sometimes it was the milkman angrily banging on the door expecting payment for his latest two pint semi-skimmed delivery, or sometimes she awoke to the blazing stereo of the next door sound system pumping away at full volume, owned by a pair of mischievous trouble makers who liked nothing better than disturbing the poor gal's beauty sleep. But either way and for whatever reason, she was woken up. Thus, came forth big black bags that appeared beneath her pretty blue ones, and Jackie grew tired and lifeless from her continued restless nights. The question she found herself asking morning or noon, was whether she would ever get the sleep she so desperately needed?

Whether she would wake up and find herself in the arms of the Lancelot of whom she dreamt. Or whether she would just wake up and find out that it was all a dream. Find out and see...

3 : JoJo the Thief

My story starts with a man who was different from the rest. JoJo stood out from the crowd not so much for his attributes so much as for what he was not. He was not particularly good at anything in fact.

Born as an orphan, or at least found washed up on a beach as a child, he had little recollection of his past. Save for a miserable upbringing in a strict dormitory-like accommodation where the diet was exclusively gruel and bedtime were a punctual eight sharp.

So, from an unhappy child, he grew into an unpleasant man. What few friends he had made in his youth now seemed to be going places, be it travelling the world, creating enterprising new careers, or bringing up families, whereas JoJo had fallen smack on the chops.

He did once apply for the prestigious role of road sweeper, only to be turned down at the interview on account of his unkempt appearance. So, if you will please imagine, he was not a happy bunny. All he could do was dream.

His dreams lacked clarity but made up for this with a tremendous sense of belonging and color. He dreamt of times and places far beyond his own meager imperfect existence (in what seemed to be an otherwise perfect world).

What's more he had flashbacks of strangers becoming friends, and memories of other lives to which he could only vaguely associate with himself at all. On occasion he had visions of the future and these gave him powers greater than any ordinary man could expect to wield.

So, this ordinary man, was in fact beneath the surface, remarkable in his own little ways. The first thing he ever did in life was steal.

He would wander the countryside spying out remarkable looking stately homes and pounce upon them with the ferocity of a tiger and the cunning of a fox, once he had decided that they held something worth stealing inside. Then he would creep up to the door and knock on it pretending to be either a double-glazing salesman, a loft insurance specialist, or a water board canvasser.

Upon opening, he often found a strictly unimpressed homeowner, but then he would redouble his efforts with tones such as :

'Here, here sir. Have you imagined what a new loft would feel like? How much happier you and your family would be? Well definitely a little warmer.'

So, with this sly tongue he often found himself sat in the sitting room, checking out the family's inheritance.

Next Joe would usually excuse himself to the bathroom where upon he would note the buildings architectural layout. Then his most common ploy was to leave the window open so that he might climb back through it later that same day, with the aid of his trusty step ladder.

Other tricks included stealing the front door key from the security pot left in the kitchen or opening the back door and getting in that way. JoJo was a clever thief. He used to enter buildings and claim items as his own not by stealth or deception but on the back of his inner wisdom. This was how he stole to the detriment of others. Using his deep inner wisdom for personal gain, despite what they say (that you must never do that). Then one day he came across a peaceful little house with a peacock painted on the front door. Walking up to it, he knocked twice and did so with evil intentions in his heart. When it opened, he jumped inside crying.

'Aha' and 'Your money or your life.'

To which the little lady who opened it was quite taken aback and at a loss for words. But just before she gave him all their money, her husband stopped her and beseeched :

'Halt villain. Desist from this ill-advised endeavor, else thou shall taste the steel of my blade!'

To which the thief replied, 'Now you want mercy, but I will give you none.' With which the two locked into a bitter struggle, metal against metal, sweat and blood mingled awash, until exhausted and exhausted the thief relented. Bleeding heavily JoJo stole away into the darkness of the night empty-handed.

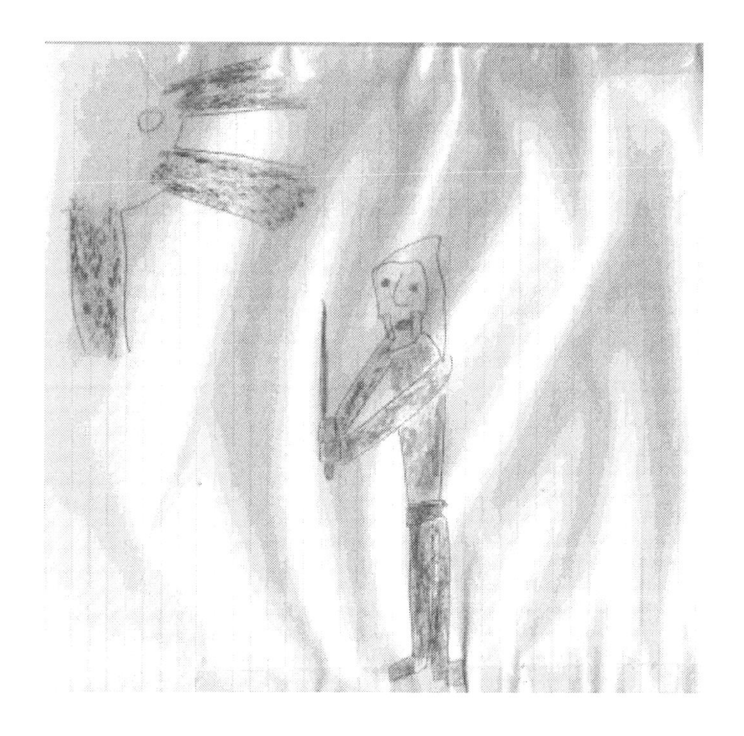

Mr. Qu lived in a little hut at the base of a mountain in China. One day he was paid a visit by the local thief, JoJo, but was damned to find an empty hut, and so he left empty-handed.

'It is a pity I could not give him our beautiful moon,' Qu finished.

There once was a thief. Who preyed on his victims with a very clever intellect indeed? He would steal not rubies or diamonds but more important things such as faith and happiness. So that when he had visited, he left his subjects feeling miserable and forlorn. And this thief never showed any emotion whatsoever.

One day he discovered a small cottage at the base of a mountain, and on knocking at the door, he was startled to discover the proprietor dressed in a full red and black traditional Samurai costume. But before he was chopped to shreds, the owner threw his wallet forward at him shouting 'Take it you fiend!' and slammed the door in his face.

With this our thief was slightly taken aback to be sure, but on regaining his composure, realized that he had gained at least one prize for which he had sought, the owner's wallet.

However, on opening it he discovered nothing inside but a rusty old two pence piece, which he chucked over his shoulder in disgust, thinking that such small change was not worth the metal it was stamped on. He realized then that by discarding our sovereign's head in such a way, he was duly signing his own death warrant, in days to come.

One dark evening when Mr. Yu was sitting in his lounge reading, he heard the quiet tip-tip-tap of a mouse under the floorboards trying to get in, or at least what he thought was a mouse. Then in a flash and without warning, the whole of his back wall came crashing down around him.

Left standing there was a slightly startled and not too happy looking burglar (Joe). Instinctively Yu went for his sabre, but the thief cried out : 'Your money or your life.'

Then Yu saw the desperate look in the eyes of a man who knows not what he does and so should not be held responsible for his actions. With this he relented : 'Take the money you fiend,' he cried, JoJo did and was gone.

The next day like clockwork Yu heard a loud banging on his front door, and on opening it discovered two middle-aged and slightly balding gentlemen standing before him.

'We're the police,' they barked 'We heard you were robbed by the treacherous night-owl last night. We'll catch that villain, and when we do...' they said suggesting the worst.

But Yu turned the whole conversation around with, 'Officers, there seems to be mistake. You see yesterday evening I was visited by an old friend, and I actually gave him my cash as a present.'

Well they couldn't very well continue to pursue the thief after that and so they were forced to call off the chase. Meaning that little Joe got away with it (again).

So, using these dubious means, Joe found himself able to steal all sorts from his neighbors. This kind of behavior was, not looked too kindly upon. So, our thief found himself forced to move from sit-in to bed-sit on account of the bad vibes he continually found knocking at his doorstep. Usually in the form of a police inquiry.

Fortunately, they never caught him. Until today. Today, they had a raid, and JoJo was busted. Someone had tipped him off. Or tipped the police off about him rather I should say. Perhaps a browser of his dodgy auction rooms had noticed an item which looked remarkably like something they used to own. Until on closer inspection they realized that it was something they used to own. Or perhaps a buyer had questioned the authenticity of one of his original paintings and taken the matter into their own hands.

4 : Short Stories

A young fighter called Joe asked his Lord :

'Our warriors and heroes have fought many battles and slain many demons. Lightning never strikes twice, and fire burns the rotten wood. The sun lifts the day from its eternal abyss and returns it there once more when the day is done. So why then do I dream nightmares? My work becomes my slavery and talking just torments?'

The old man said, 'Seek out the truth within, and you'll find it all about.'

Mr. Hong Ling was a stout man with a big heart. He never wanted to be rich or famous, save that for the kings and celebrities, all he wanted was to be happy.

Whenever Mr. Hong met a rich man he would smile, bow his head, and ask for a little change, then was on his way. He also used to buy sweets and toys for the children and in this way came to be known as the laughing monk.

One day, a little caterpillar bumped into a big ugly giant.

'Oh dear,' the giant cried. 'How do you manage all those little legs when I have difficulty with just these two?'

'Actually, I don't,' the caterpillar replied rather smugly, 'they manage themselves.'

Two young Zen Warriors, Mubi and Hani Yuecheng, were invited to pay homage to a local king in the Taipei district of southern China. After arriving at his palace and knocking on the big oak door they were both shown in to a comfortable and luxurious seating area.

'Your Majesty,' Mubi started, 'I have never seen such a well preserved and decorated place in all my years! Yours must surely be the greatest kingdom on the face of this earth!'

This was followed by a minute's silence at which point his companion Yuecheng declared :

'I don't think this place is all that great! I can see mice holes in the floorboards and cobwebs under the chandeliers!'

Upon which, they were both shown out by the imperial guards.

The old Ye called out to himself every day, 'Master!' When he answered, 'Yes sir?'

Then, 'Stop smoking and drinking,' 'Yes sir.' 'and listen to other people's advice.' 'Yes sir, yes sir,' he would finish.

Joe asked a monk, 'I have just entered the monastery – please teach me.'

The monk said, 'Have you eaten rice porridge today?' JoJo said that he had. Then the monk said, 'Well you had better wash your bowl.'

Old man David would clap his hands together and shout, 'No!' whenever his children wanted anything. This seemed to quieten them for a while. Until one day when little Benjamin ran to him hoping for a glass of orange. Then realizing his mistake, the boy quickly put up his own finger and said, 'No!'

Once upon a time a little child ran crying to an old woman. 'Help me, mother,' she cried.

'My parents are breaking up, and I don't know what to do.' The old woman took her hand and said, 'Be patient my child, the storm will pass.'

A long time ago lived two little friends. Mu played the harp while May listened. But one day May fell sick and died. So, from that day forth Mu cut the strings and never played again.

One cloudy day her friend asked Piao Liang Hua (translated as Pretty Flower) : 'Where is the sun?' 'It's sleeping,' Piao Liang Hua replied.

Ten men sat basking in the sun one day, before it hid behind the clouds. Then a woman stood up and told them :

'One of you has been writing me amorous letters. I don't mind reading them; in fact, I find it amusing really, to hear what one of you really feels about me. However, I think my husband would have something to say about it if he found out, and I have a good mind to let him know if it continues. So, I'll ask you, either the perpetrator step forward now, else forever hold your peace.'

No one dared do so, but from that day forth, she never again received another such letter.

Two young monks were sitting out in the garden one day when they saw a pair of butterflies frolicking amongst the marigolds.

'Hey,' asked the younger of the two. 'Do you suppose it is the insect that moves, or the wind that moves it?'

But the other monk just shrugged his shoulders.

Joey and Michael were two monks out for a walk one day, when they came across a young damsel in distress. She was stranded on a rock with high flood waters all around. Instantly the monks leapt into action, Joey making a bridge from an old fallen tree, which Michael carried the girl across on his shoulders, to safety. Sometime later, after they had bid farewell, Joey turned to his companion and said :

'You know as monks; we're not supposed to touch women.'

To which the other frowned and said, 'Yes, but whilst I left her on the bank you are still carrying her.'

One day the venerable emperor went to his brother and asked him for help.

'Tea,' he said. 'I have travelled far and wide across deserts and seas, but I still search. Where can I find this treasure which I seek?'

'Ha!' laughed his brother. 'What you want is not mine to give!'

The emperor respected his brother even more from that day on. So that when he began to fall asleep in between their lessons, his brother would just retire to his chamber and let the other get the rest his body was asking for.

Sue was a country bumpkin who discovered some monks sitting by a fire engaged in a heated discussion.

'Fire is an elemental property,' the first raged. 'Nothing can stand in its way!' followed by :

'Rubbish, fire like all the elements, is but a fragment of the universal mind/imagination, and that is INSUBSTANTIAL.'

Whereupon little Suzie stepped forward and entered the fray.

'What do you think?' the monks asked her. 'I think,' she said, 'that if the fire exists in your mind, it must be hot in there!'

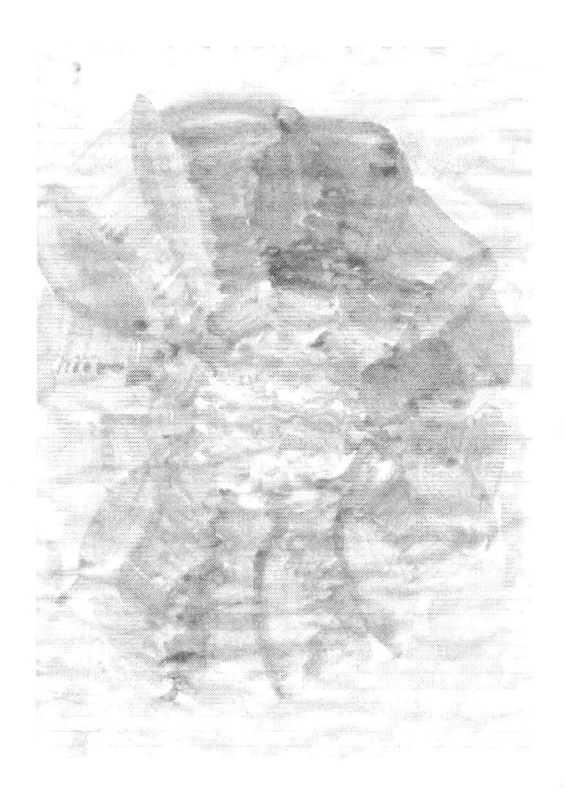

Josephine was a little gnome who liked sitting in the garden. Sometimes it would shine and sometimes it would rain but she liked it whatever it was. One day a gentle rain filled the air, and then a moment later a rainbow burst from behind a cloud. She thought she could hear heaven whisper to her :

'Thanks for your discourse on God's dharma, my child.'

But I haven't said anything, she thought, and as she did so a breeze filled the sky with flowers.

One day a long time ago little Jo caught her friends arguing over a little kitten they had found. Julie and Samantha claimed it was theirs because they had found it, whereas Cindy and Sandy said by rights the cat belonged to them because she had been found on their patch. At this point, Jim produced a pair of scissors and offered to cut it in two, in order that they might both have a piece!

One day a spider bumped into a big ugly cyclops. ‘Oh, woe is me’ the giant cried. ‘How can you manage all those little legs when I have difficulty with just these two!’

5 : Reflections

Where's the safest place for the most precious things? Before I sting you with my answer, I want to explain how I got there.

I once had a fine collection of antiques. Great powerful items but having them overwhelmed me to the point where I broke down and got rid of them and a great deal of what was going right in my life for me at that time. Such a waste. Despite my dad's protestations to the contrary, the large silver Buddha, old scroll depicting one hundred tigers, and red/green jade sword, were all old and good (and valuable!).

I also collected a big songbook with old and new favorites. I even destroyed this. Now there are still more antiques out there. There is an argument that by destroying some, I have only made the others that bit more precious. In this way, I have buried my presents in antiquity, but this is a defeatist way of looking at things. Part of me feels defeated in this respect. My life hasn't worked out according to plan, but that's another story.

Songs can be rewritten and re-sung. Antiques can be re-made, and monuments re-founded. Heroes reborn and lovers re-loved. Surely that's the greatest antique of them all?

What does it take to climb a mountain? I don't know because I never have. But I've read about men who did. (Maurice Herzog in Annapurna). If you forget his nationality for a minute (: French) and concentrate on his achievement, you will see that he was the leader of a team who scaled the rock. Despite placing himself in the thick of it, and coming first to the top, nowadays, mountaineers don't always head the battle. Or a leader can choose to lead from inside the group formation.

What this would have meant for Herzog, would have been that he as an individual would not have reached the top. Would have held back and let one of the others get the trophy. As it happened on the descent, their mountaineering team rushed in fear of the monsoon, and two of the climbers hurt themselves with severe frostbite and subsequent amputations as a result.

Despite the remarkable first Herzog achieved; it wasn't without injury. So, was this it? Is second place just as good? Or what about last? Surely, it's not the winning or losing but taking part that counts? Mind you, Herzog did it with a team, of at least a dozen men, and that is ultimately where the achievement lies.

The powerful hero, Yong Hong, believed in the power of love. He approached the great unclimbable mountain with feelings of hope and dread. After climbing for days, he stood at the foot of a near vertical glacier as high as the eye could see, apparently cradling heaven itself. 'So, this is what it means to climb a mountain', he thought. Then he took out his ice axe, checked that his harness was securely in place and began the ascent. After climbing a hundred treacherous feet, he reached another obstacle, a demon's claw outstretched. He surmounted this one only by the skin of his teeth, and it wasn't over then.

Another hour's climbing lay ahead, until at last with his face drenched in sweat, and his body burning up in the heat of its own exertion, he realized that he had done it. He had made it, reached the summit, and in this final hour achieved all of which he had ever sought.

The journey down passed un-eventfully enough, and once he was safely in the arms of his favorite local tavern at base camp, he reflected that perhaps he was stupid for having attempted the climb in the first place, but certainly he was stronger for having done it as a result.

At this point, Joe stood up and said, 'Enough. Enough of your babblings. I want to go out and discover the world for myself!' And so, he packed his bags and left.

He had reached a point in life where he felt he had to overcome the worst mishaps which he had been faced with, and it was time to move on. He still felt like he had a couple of karmic obligations to pursue, that is apologies to make, and demons to conquer, so then addictions to overcome, but despite all this he just felt like leaving.

However, no sooner than he had made it to the front door, a man stepped in front of him.

'Sit down Jimmy,' he said, 'you're going nowhere'. So, JoJo sat back down, and Ren continued :

'This reminds me of a young man I once knew called Great Waves, (or Da Lang in Chinese). He started life out as a street wrestler, and he wasn't half a bad one at that. On his good days he would round up all the scum and trash from the street, put them in a half-nelson and then pile-drive them to oblivion.

However, on a bad day he would be trounced, and he found children, even little girls walking all over him. Well clearly this was a degrading spectacle for a fully grown man to endure, but no matter how many wrestling manuals he read, or old WWF and WCW tapes he watched, he couldn't seem to correct his technique and shore up the holes...

Then one day he heard about a wise old man who lived halfway up a mountain who might be able to help him. Well having already reached his wits end, Great Waves set out to find out whatever possibly it was this old guy could teach him. And for days and nights he endured the harsh sun and freezing moon, until eventually he fell upon a little shack perched in the middle of nowhere. Sure, that this could not be the right place, he stopped to ask the proprietor for directions.

'Kind sir, please help me, I'm looking for a great warrior.' The little man shook his head :

'Wars do not make one great! Help you I will but feed me you must.'

So Great Waves proceeded to share some of his rations out with the elder. The old man then told him that what he was seeking was inside himself, and that all he had to do was meditate. Lang tried and it worked. He closed his eyes and counted to ten and let the world drift away, leaving only the ebb and flow of the great sea with all the little people swimming in it.

Then he turned around and thanked the old man, before making his way back home.

Once he had eventually reached his base, he tried out his new moves, the Klingon Stun gun, and the Romulan Screwdriver, which the old man on the mountain had also shown him in a spare minute, and they worked.

Then one morning after the wrestler woke up, nothing remained where his little hut once stood, but the ebb and flow of the great sea. In this way he saw true to his namesake and became the greatest wrestler in all of China.

6 : Smoking

How then, reflected JoJo, can I do good if I don't have the muscles of Heracles or the speed of a cheetah. Is there some other way? This contemplation was just too much for him. He had to sit down and have another cigarette. JoJo did this but felt nothing.

Or at least he didn't feel that he was falling back into the trap of the addiction. But then when he gave into the urge before it wasn't giving into anything. Precisely that. He had achieved nothing. Rather smoking, and to a lesser extent chewing gum, is an anti-achievement. By smoking that one he was now faced with a dilemma. Does he own up to the world and admit smoking one, or deny this to them and himself, and thereby preserve his sense of honor and self-integrity. Or rather by lying, he would be acting somewhat to undo this.

Something told him not to tell, and in a strange way preserving trust was another value which he also held dear. However, seeing as he had relapsed today, he also vowed to do something else good today. He also felt angry at himself and was determined not to have any more.

Should he use any means possible to preserve the valuable innocence? No, not yet. Just certain means. But what? So now the trial was to see how long he could go for without being a snitch.

Joe was left with nothing. Save for the waves lapping at his feet and the sun shining on his back, the kid was all alone. Abandoned by the world which had raised him, he had never felt so low. This is when he reached for that other little monster, the cigarette. The drug which systematically destroys a person's health, looks, and finance, all in search of a quick fix.

Yeah, James Dean smoked, our kid would justify to himself. But what did Mr. Dean die of? Lung cancer, I think. Exactly. Unfortunately, Joe was neither inclined nor disposed to listen to this little fact, let alone hear it. And so, he smoked, at first five a day, then ten, then fifteen, all the way trying to feel good and increasingly forgetting how to. So that when the day finally came that he had had enough, and he smoked his final fag, he had weeks if not months of restless nights and early mornings ahead of him, all the while craving, dreaming even, of lighting up.

But if our kid was anything, he was bloody minded. He did suffer, but he also read to keep his mind at bay. And he wrote a little to temper his fingers. So that with the gun of faith and a sprinkle of good luck, he was finally able to kill the filthy beast in its tracks.

When I stopped smoking, I had to break something (the addiction). Now this thing needed to be broken just as hard. But as I've already mentioned, I wanted to preserve my integrity while doing so. I must remember that I shouldn't have done it, and that is the main thing. I can now understand why some smokers get quite cross when offered a cigarette. It wasn't for them a risk that they would fall into the nicotine trap. It's the knowledge that they've already fallen into the trap before, making it a possible certainty. Any urge to smoke is a negative urge, and hence should be regarded in such light consecutively.

Maybe, I contemplated, I ought to read some more of that precious book which helped me quit smoking in the first place (Allen Carr, 1987). That should do it. Now where have I left it? The next day, I visited my doctor's surgery and asked him for treatment. 'I've brought you some stories,' he said. 'Now sit down and listen'...

7 : War

It's funny how time can just slip by, JoJo reflected. One minute everything can be going as normal and the next, and for completely no reason of your own, your destiny is taken from beneath your feet and you find yourself hurtling down a toboggan run at God knows what speed, with no brakes in sight, and not knowing when it will end. This happened to me when I was incarcerated, but I imagine a very similar experience is happening right now to those poor souls trapped in Iraq. Norman Kemp, I think his name is. Anyway, my heart goes out to him; it really does. Having embarked on a peace mission in that God forsaken war zone, and then finding himself caught up in the thick of it, beggars' belief.

Although I can see the argument against going there, that in no way forgives the terrorists' actions. I get quite tired in justifying either side's score on the battle. The invaders, led by G. Bush who has quite recently apologized for going to war on false information (there were no Weapons of Mass Destruction after all), or the invaded, here being represented by a previously unheard of group called the swords

of righteousness, who don't get my sympathy at all.

But this is turning into one hot cookie which I have already mentioned, not how I feel sympathy for terrorists. So, before I end up offending too many people's sensibilities I want to get back to the narrative.

The struggle between Philosophy and Religion is one which we all should consider. As is that of work and play. Each of these fields seems to have an opposite. So, the opposite of religion is philosophy and the opposite of work is play. Or how about the opposite of religion is atheism and the opposite of philosophy is stupidity. The opposite of work being laziness and play being misery.

I think the four above mentioned fields go a long way to both explain and describe the major areas of life. Football being a cross between playing hard and working hard too, music more play, hard graft pure work and love pure play even if it doesn't always feel that way, but there are clear conflicts between the divides. You will tend to find hardcore religious nuts discounting philosophy with the ease of a sigh, and professors of certain philosophical matters equally rubbishing religious truths with the effort of a laugh. Just as hard-core religious states are about as far from sitting at the table with communist ones, as chalk is of resembling cheese on a plate. That's not to say there aren't elements within these political systems which deviate from the party line. Just as Dadaism (a free going crazy British social movement which stressed creative deviation) differed from Thatcherism (the right-wing political trend of the time). In the same way as Kurt Cobain's Nirvana differed from all forms of music, be it pop or rock, and I suppose Sid Vicious' the Sex Pistols did a generation before.

So, the hidden Sufi within the moderate Muslim may reject the statute books of his state's law, when he sees a personal truth, or element of mercy in a particular given situation. Likewise, a state obliging Chinese person may embrace a free market perspective in each situation to get the job done, much as the minister Deng Xiaoping has done with regards to opening their country's economy. Even if the rural, agrarian nature of much of China's industry remains.

So, what is the solution we might ask? Our state here in this country is far from perfect. I don't think there is a single system or economy which can solve all the problems. The solution must be a combination of the many. So, what's that – democracy? More like diversity, I'd say!

One day a young officer, Clifford, went out for a picnic on the fertile lush Indian plains. Halfway through however, he spotted a tiger who spotted him also. Before he knew it, he was running for his life, the tiger hot on his heels. Then he came across the edge of a precipice and hesitated, the whole of his life flashed before his eyes.

Before the frantic man was able to catch his breath, he grabbed hold of the nearest wild vine to swing through the trees (much like a Tarzan of the 90s). But the good plan turned pear-shaped when the vine stopped swinging and he was lost dangling there with nowhere else to turn.

At this point, he spotted a red strawberry growing on a branch nearby and reaching out, he was just able to pick it. My, how sweet it tasted.

:Transcribed from an old Buddhist legend.

Guan Yu was a famous general in ancient China. So great was his might that he came to be known amongst his people as the God of War.

One day he returned home to his mum, having had his fill of fighting, and said to her :

'I've had enough! I want to leave the army and become a thespian!'

With which she scolded him and ordered him to visit their local tattooist. There he would have the map of China cut into his back, to always remind him of his priority (to the country!)

One day a long time ago, a division of the Japanese imperial army went out on patrol. They dropped by Mr. Xiao sheng's temple hoping for something to eat, but when they discovered the gruel he had put in their bowls, they threw it on the floor and demanded better food.

The abbot of the temple was unfazed by this and said, 'So sorry if our food isn't good enough for you. Please feel free to go to another restaurant.'

An old farmer once discovered that his prize stallion had run away. Distraught, he looked all over for it but to no avail. So, feeling unhappy, he sat himself atop a bundle of hay. His neighbor Jack passed by and offered his condolences.

The next day the farmer was happy to see that his horse had returned accompanied by five fine young mares. Together they frolicked about in the fields and when his neighbor popped by, this time he gave his congratulations.

Imagine then the farmer's shock when on the following day his youngest son fell off one of the new horses while breaking her in. This was also a shock to the boy who was rushed to hospital where he was forced to stay for a miserable six weeks, to give time for his bones to heal. That evening Jack dropped by to send his condolences again.

On the fourth day, the farmer was surprised to be visited by a local sergeant major who was recruiting for a push in the international war effort. With tears in his eyes the farmer mentioned that his son was in no fit state to fight, and sadly wouldn't be able to go. But he was secretly relieved at the outcome to the end of what had been a most bizarre chain of events.

Silver was a warrior who for years had fought in the ranks of armies against evil tyrants and warlords, under tall night shade grasses and on arid desert plains. But now he was old, and his legs were weary. Whilst the sun still shone with its same golden splendor and the birds still sang in the air, our man could no longer touch his toes without pulling about every muscle in his back. As for the army, well you could just forget about it.

Sitting in the shade of the olive trees, he reflected :

'As I grow older what have I lost? What have I gained? The love of nature and an affinity with fellow human beings which was not so before. Flattered by the yellow sun as we are, all living beings' birds, bugs, and trees even, are given our moment of life on this planet. This is our gift and salvation too. Don't forsake them...

8 : Fencing

Fighting in the dark like a rat in a cage or a pig in a rut – and it's pitch black. I cannot see my enemy, only hear him, at night when the clock strikes twelve, but I can't hear the clock, only my own heartbeat. This would suggest that my enemy is closer than I would like to think. He listens to my every breath. That brother I told you about, is he my enemy? Don't be ridiculous. I don't like him, but he just keeps me contained. And then when I escape his cage will I be free? Well, I think I will carry on fighting. Fighting an invisible ghost with invisible punches. Punches for freedom. Revolutionary punches in a naked world. Put some clothes on please, I cry to him, and he listens somewhat. I could say that he listens to every word I say, but it would be a lie. Yet I fear he precisely hears those words I would prefer that he did not.

So then is he deaf? Only as deaf as I have been for all these years. He can count on his strengths (virility, industry, meat) and me mine (abstinence, laziness, and vegetables). Even though I have burnt down my own home to see his back. But can I? Unfortunately, I can't. Instead I only stumble.

A long time ago, an ancient jewel was stolen from the crown of a universal monarch and embedded in the spear of an angry warlord. He used the spear to fight and eventually defeat the armies of the once proud man and claim his lands as his own.

The spear was forgotten about as the years went by, and now remains only in the memories of a few folk and their occasional fireside stories.

One sad and soggy morning when digging technology had excavated into the heart of a pyramid previously untouched, a diamond was found, and a beautiful crown constructed around it. This was claimed by a shadowy rogue who, emerging from the darkness, deemed that only the most honest or foolhardy man had the right to challenge him for it.

Eventually they came, from all corners of the earth, to claim their right to the sacred jewel in the crown. Which had the power of making the wearer into the most beautiful woman, assuming of course it was a woman that had it.

The first two fighters to claim the diamond were once brothers now separated at birth. One a businessman, the other a tramp. One wore suits, the other rags. So, each of them fought for the prize, but there were others.

JoJo was the son of an epic Samurai warrior, the Dying Phoenix. His dad was admired across the land for his weapon skills, especially his staff fighting and defense. He in turn had learnt these from his dad.

On one random Sunday afternoon, JoJo turned to his dad and asked him to teach him everything he knew. His dad paused and then asked him to come back later that day. So later, in the afternoon the boy did just that and this time the Dying Phoenix told him to return in a month.

A month later and the boy returned and asked the same question again. This time when he asked for instruction, his old man scolded him and said :

'How can I teach my own son? Never.'

With which JoJo was thoroughly admonished. Rather than give up trying, he set forth on a concentrated program of energy building movements and cardiovascular exercises, so that a year later when he approached the Samurai again he was able to do so with his head held high.

Yet again the Phoenix disagreed saying; 'I can't teach you, offspring!'

With which, the youngster relented. This time instead of devoting his time to combat skills, he decided to let others do the fighting. JoJo instead worked domestically in the house.

Cooking, cleaning and especially gardening. Doing the little things which left undone can become a major eyesore, such as sweeping the leaves up, cutting the grass and pruning the hedges. In this way, JoJo never did become a great Samurai like his dad. He became something else instead : he became a gardener.

'What else can we talk about JoJo?' said Ren (his new best friend). 'I know,' he said, 'let's talk about the garden!' replied JoJo. 'Oh,' said Ren.

'You know, I used to love going to gardening shops and choosing flowers and plants that looked nice, and then planting them in the ground, but what I especially loved was watching the flowers bud and then blossom. Be they daffodils, chrysanthemums, tulips, marigolds, lupins, red hot pokers, or even a viola.'

'That's nice,' exonerated Ren. 'I think I know those plants, and I bet the birds like them too.'

'I don't know about the birds, but the butterflies certainly do,' retorted JoJo.

'So, what about plants then?' he asked him.

'Yeah, plants are good,' he said, 'except for weeds. I can't stand the little blighters. They get all over my flower bed if I'm not careful. Then it seems like I have to spend half of the summer digging them up!'

'Oh, that's a pity,' Ren replied. 'Can't you just use weed- killer?'

'Well, I know other gardeners use it,' JoJo replied. 'But I don't like the stuff. I don't like the idea of spraying my nice organic soil, rich with worms and creepy crawlies or what-have-you, with what is in effect poison. No thank you. I'll stick to my spade and trowel thanks.'

9 : Prison

As JoJo spied the silent and unmarked police car pull up outside his house, he knew his game was up. So rather than run, he opened the door, put his hands above his head and was led away.

Inside, JoJo had lots of time on his hands, and one of the first things he set about doing was writing stories and poems. What's more, he listened to the varied and vivid tales the other prisoners had to tell and wrote them down. These ranged from jungle stories to mountainous ones, from city adventures to the desert expeditions, and everyone he scribed to paper with his faithful quill and black ink.

One day one of the guards, on noticing this inmate's curious scribblings, stopped nearby to peer over his shoulder and catch a glimpse of whatever it was he might be writing. And upon reading a story, he chuckled out loud and smiled a big smile as if to say, ‘nice one mate’.

JoJo’s time was not reduced on account of his writings. It just seemed that way. His stint in jail was debatably the worst period of his life, but it wasn’t until he got out, he was able to really notice the difference.

In jail, JoJo had a moment of revelation. He discovered a side to him that he never knew had existed. Or rather he had suspected, feared even, that it was there. But he had always tried to deny it, to refuse to acknowledge its existence and in that way starve the damn thing of oxygen and thus kill it.

Still, prisons are so built that the rats always come crawling from deep within the woodwork, and the submerged nasty monsters rear their dirty heads, and begin to feed. This monster was a forgiving monster. One that forgave everything JoJo had once held in contempt and sought to begin anew.

That meant the army were forgiven for their foreign atrocities, the politicians for their political ones, and even miscreant authors who had penned what he would previously have regarded as literary rubbish, were all forgiven.

But this little monster was still a monster nonetheless, and so it forced JoJo to retreat on everything he had so dearly felt for all those years. He also laughed at himself simultaneously and took great pride in watching the poor man undo himself.

There was one man who seemed different to JoJo. This fella kept himself to himself but was not bothered by the vagabonds who populated half of the cells. He neither asked for nor was demanded of, protection money which was unusual for someone of his stature within the prison hierarchy.

One day JoJo approached him and, feeling a wave of religious awe and aura overcome him, asked

'Why did the enlightened one, known to you and me as Buddha, leave India and settle in Tibet?'

Ren Yuecheng grumbled something about the tea being too watery and was about to fall back to sleep before JoJo shouted at him : 'Answer Me!' With which Mr. Ren looked up and after a time muttered :

'An oak tree grows strong over the summer months but come winter then even that must shed its leaves.

And in a few hundred years even that will die altogether. There that is why.'

To which JoJo skulked away, thinking that either he didn't fully understand the answer, or that Ren Cheng was just a con artist.

A minute later, displeased with the fruit of his labor, JoJo returned to the monk and tried again this time with :

'Oh, great one, I have of times late, befallen great misfortune and trouble upon myself. Please help me. Can you show me a way out of this maze, or at least give me a word of advice to that effect?'

'Ha!' Ren Yuecheng said and nothing more. It seemed that JoJo was going to have to find a way out of the maze on his own!

Ren Cheng sat facing a wall when another inmate approached him and asked :

'Please help me?'

'Whatever is the matter sir?' Ren inquired.

'It's my wife,' the other said. 'On finding out I'm in here, she's left me for this other guy. He's handsome, kind, good looking, all the things that I'm not. Oh, whatever should I do?'

'Dear me' Ren replied. 'I could tell you to chill out and relax, but I doubt it would make any difference. I think she's clearly taken on this random trajectory and all we can do is sit back and watch. If it makes any difference to you, I can tell you that my first wife did the same thing, and I got over it. We always do.'

‘Probably the best advice I can offer you is don’t fret. Try and make the most of a bad situation. If she’ll return your calls, talk to her. If she won’t, then leave your phone turned on anyway just in case she does. And if she doesn’t, just chill.'

'Staying cool in a moment of chaos is a sure sign of a hero but feeling loss in the case of a split means you’re human. Even heroes must be human, from time to time.'

There are certain benefits to being inside, JoJo thought to himself one day. Sure, the food sucks, but at least you get fed regularly, three meals a day. The lack of women is a problem, but there’s certainly no shortage of male compatriots (fraternity). Not that I would count them as friends, not many of them at least.

Being behind the four walls does provide you with a united enemy with which to oppose, and the time spent inside also allows you to flush out the rubbish from your previously jam-packed schedule and start a new slate. I'm not saying I like it in here, I don't. I hate it with all my heart.

All I'm saying that is, given the initial cooling off period which can last anywhere up to twelve months, and you can begin, (even if all-be-it piece by piece) to see the bigger picture.

Well, JoJo thought, Ren Yuecheng is one friend I've made. I've also learnt not to mess with authority because they have infinite reserves of manpower behind them, so to speak. And I've also learned that despite being on the wrong side of the fence, the law is there for a reason, and demands respect in and as of itself. This was something which I didn't appreciate before.

Being inside also gives one a chance to think and reflect. So, while there is surely such a thing as thinking and reflecting too much, a little from time to time never did anybody any harm. It also gives me a chance to write and tell stories. Like this one :

The next day JoJo called Ren over and told him :

'Buddy listen to me. I'm bored of sitting here facing these same damn walls day on day. I want to get out here, and I want you to help me.'

Ren just shook his head and said :

'Sorry mate. We're in a high security prison cell, the only way either of us is leaving is in a number of years once our time is up, or if either of us croaks it.'

'Damn,' said JoJo, and 'thanks.'

But they didn't die and were released eventually. Then when he (JoJo) had a chance to breathe the fresh blue air from the outside sky, he sat down, and he wrote about it. He wrote about his time inside, the people he'd met and the things they'd got up to together. Slightly dull perhaps, but compelling nonetheless once you get into it.

He wrote about things he heard, things he'd made up, things he thought he'd heard and things he never did hear. He wrote about people he'd met, people he wished he'd met, people he never did meet, and people he'd dreamt about meeting. So, this is that book.

The next day JoJo went to his uncle Ren's cell from across the block. Having just been granted movement within the prison on good behavior grounds, he wasn't sure how his friend would receive him, so he was relieved when he was greeted with a smile and invited in to share a nice cup of cold water.

'My my, you'll never be a warrior our lad.' Ren chided him in betwixt sips.

'Never, never, never.'

'Thanks,' JoJo considered as he drank his tea but not without the slightest enthusiasm.

'My Art, now there was a fighter. Strong as a bear and fast as a fox. My, he'd knock you for six and still have time to catch the end of EastEnders.'

'Well I'll never.' JoJo stumbled over his words now.

'Oh, you will, or rather he would,' Ren went on. 'God rest his soul.'

'But whatever happened to the poor kid?' JoJo tentatively inquired.

'To our Artania, now I could write a book on that alone. You still sure you're interested? Well here, ask one of the lags to get me another cup of water and I'll tell yer...'

'It all kicked off on his eighteenth birthday, when by a stroke of luck his Uncle Peterson returned from an overseas military expedition to the far east. Far from bringing glad tidings, and despite joy at meeting his nephew again after what had been a considerable number of years, the old man was filled with grave forebodings.

'I bring bad news,' Peterson told us.

'The enemies of the king are amassing, and we're going to need every man we've got to stave off defeat.' So, Art turned to his father, who had long since been immobilized from a near fatal back injury and asked for his advice. 'Do as your will determine,' Art's senior answered. 'You're eighteen now, and that's old enough to join the army.'

At this point our kid hesitated. On the one hand his sense of honor and pride drew him towards defending his kingdom and loved ones in it, but on the other, a grave foreboding regarding any kind of killing engulfed his conscience and very nearly overwhelmed him. Let alone prevented him from signing up.

The next thing he could remember was the city's great war trumpets echoing out throughout the land and David stood there, on his great war chariot during it all. In the distance, he could see the enemy's armies amassing, and besides and behind him he spied his allies and kinsmen armed and ready for war. Now it was his old uncle Peterson who, not yet fully rested from his recent expedition, leapt astride a great white horse and, having donned his mighty iron breastplate, lifted the herald into the enemy's ranks. Peterson however was neither as nimble nor as strong as he used to be, and it was only what seemed like a matter of moments later before he was struck by a crossbow bolt smack between the eyes and killed outright.

This infuriated Artania, who took the reins to the stallion and spurred it forwards into the encroaching scoundrels. With this, the allies held their breath, but were relieved to watch the son pluck up the fallen banner and carry on. He neither looked back nor hesitated in his courage.

It wasn't until later on in the afternoon, when the main battle was over and only the carrying away of the casualties remained, did Art reflect that his uncle's actions may well have been foolish; certainly they were foolhardy, but they were brave above all else. He inscribed on his uncle's tombstone.

'Here lies a brave man : Peterson'.

'So, you think that I'm a scumbag?' JoJo asked his friend, Ren Yuecheng, one damp, overcast afternoon.

'Not exactly,' Ren replied. 'I just think that it must be hard for any man to conduct a civilized, let alone respectable life, given the amount of careless disrespect for the law which you've taken upon yourself.'

'I can see your point,' JoJo replied, being new and reformed. 'I guess I have been rather bad in my own little way.'

'I'll say,' Ren threw back, 'but enough about you. Let me tell you about one of my relatives, Artania.'

'Do you have to?'

'Yes, I do. So, there he was an oldish chap getting himself shot down in some careless war, when all the while he could have been settling down and raising a good family much like your father, Dave, did. If it weren't for his fascination with guns and killing things I might add.'

'So anyway, back in the day before the army took him away from us, old Art was actually a half decent chap. Did you know that? A warrior monk who wandered the world, righting wrongs, and seeking out justice wheresoever he considered that it was needed. Follow me now…'

Ren led JoJo away from the communal area and into his own personal cell, wherein he pulled back a dirty rag revealing a little but perfectly formed gold statue of a warrior prince. On its brass name plate was inscribed the name Artania.

'Wow,' JoJo said. 'Is that really him?'

'Yes sir,' Ren replied. 'That's him alright. This statue was carved in commemoration of one of the bravest and most compassionate men our country has ever seen.'

'Really?' JoJo inquired, 'Tell me, what did he do?'

‘What didn’t he do?! He only saved three villages from the throes of impending perils which nobody else would have thought to help.’

‘Wow!’ JoJo just shook his head.

'The first catastrophe occurred in Egypt some twenty long years ago. The Nile had a tendency of flooding its banks at the spring equinox when the rain waters overtook the flatlands.

Back then, we didn’t have the elaborate flood plains system set up which we now have in place. Still in one year we were hit so bad that all our crops and homes were washed away. Artania, with a never-ending energy (which I’ll never understand) set about single handedly rebuilding the homes and replanting the fields.

On observing this one man's efforts, soon others joined him. Before long the whole village was working flat out on a reconstruction and rehabilitation programs devised to restore life to our stricken homes and livelihoods. Before long wheat was growing in the fields, and the villagers' homes were rebuilt, further up on the banks. Largely thanks to the effort and determination of one man.

The next disaster followed on the heels of the water catastrophe and was bred in no small amount on the backs of the dying animals which lay upon the banks, and the rats which fed on them. People started dying.

First it was just the old folk and the very young, and this was generally attributed to the harsh weather that the summer had just brought in. But then when more animals, and perfectly normal people started croaking it, alarm bells started ringing.

So, the village elders had the sensible idea of setting up quarantine zones between different parts of the village and our Artania was one of the braves who volunteered to carry essential supplies between the sectors by horseback. In this way the plague was eventually beaten, and everything was able to return to normal.

‘Wow,’ JoJo said. ‘He sounded like quite a guy.’

‘Sure was,’ Ren conceded.

‘But all of this might have been for nothing once the great Dragon set upon our village. Then some of us felt that we had had it, for sure.’

'A Dragon?' JoJo gasped. 'But I thought such things only existed in fairy tales!'

'We thought so too' Ren replied.

'But this is no fairytale! One day our precious village was attacked by one. Then the hospital nurse went missing, and we received a ransom note sent back to us on the horns of the remains of a half-eaten ram, asking for ten hundred gold pieces, which was then a lot of money (as it -is now). This was to be paid to the entrance of a cave halfway up the mountain which overlooks the village, else we could wave goodbye to our pretty little damsel!'

'Heavens!' JoJo said. 'Whatever did you do?'

'We did what any other self-respecting village would have done,' Ren replied. 'We sent our bravest and strongest young knight to fight it.'

'Wow,' JoJo said. 'And so that was uncle Art?' 'Sure was.' 'Did he win?'

'Wouldn't be much of a story if he didn't now, would it? But in any case, he did brave the flames and fire of that treacherous lizard, to pummel a stake through its heart and bring back our nurse in one piece. What a relief huh? And along with the maiden you might be interested to know that he also returned a casket of the village's treasures, gold pieces and the like, which the dragon had been hoarding up over the years.

So that my boy, is how old Artania came to save our village for the third time.'

'Wow,' JoJo gasped again. 'I wish I were a dragon.'

A long time ago in a faraway country, old Artania was asked to paint for the Emperor the words of love (in

Chinese) on an old piece of parchment given to him, but try as he might, he couldn't find the inspiration to start his work.

Then one morning he heard a single bird singing outside, and without even knowing which bird it was, this gave him the inspiration to start work. As he was painting, colours flowed freely, and soon the canvas was covered with splendid colour and details fit for a king.

Without warning, a little child entered the room carrying a glass of orange. The boy stepped up to the desk and said, 'Here, I have brought you a drink.'

The old man thanked him, drank it, and got on with his work. After that the emperor thanked him for his painting and said it was the best he had ever seen, which Artania thought was a slight exaggeration but bowed none the less and left feeling happy he had pleased his King.

10 : Asking Maya

'What can I talk to you about now?' asked Joe one nice day, sitting on a park bench with his friend Ren, some years after they both had been released.

'I'm running out of ideas.'

'Keep going,' said Ren, 'you're doing fine.'

'I know, I'll tell you about my time in hospital. I've already told you about my time in the cell, but I was in hospital too for a bit as well you know.'

'Really?' said Ren.

'Yeah, really. It's not nice going to the hospital for such a long period of time.'

'Yes, I can imagine.'

'Can you? Having your liberties taken away from you and being forced to live in such a small space over any given period of time with a group of others is really quite freaky, especially if you have grown accustomed to your independence as I have. I mean, I did make friends in there, but you must be friendly to survive that environment, I suppose. The worst thing is they want to take me back in to do some more tests.'

'Who do?' asked Ren.

'Oh, the doctors and that. They seem to think because they couldn't fix me the first time around it might be worth having another go. But you know what? I'm not having any of it – they can put their hospital where the sun doesn't shine.'

'That's a pity,' Ren finished.

'What else can you tell me about?' Ren asked JoJo.

'How about the time I was homeless?' he replied.

'Go on then,' he said.

'Oh, it's really quite simple – when you've got nowhere else to go, you hit the street,' he said.

'What does that mean?'

'It means that when, through no fault of your own, you find yourself sleeping beneath a canopy of the stars you have to start facing up to things.'

'Really, didn't you get cold?'

'Not half,' he replied. 'Chilly and wet and thoroughly miserable, but even that is better than prison.

See, I've slept rough, love, on the street in a bin on a cement slab – you name it, I've done it, or thereabouts anyway. The worst thing is the rats. Not really. It's the cold. Rats I can handle.

So anyway, there I was on the streets, but listen – it does have the occasional advantage. Like friends you make on them tend to be a lot more worthy and generous than the other variety. I mean nothing lasts forever and you get all sorts, but what I just said.'

'Can we talk about walking now?' Ren asked. 'What a good idea! Because you see I used to absolutely love walking. It's such an experience you know, and I used to walk everywhere. To college to study, to feed the horses, through the rains and hail and snow, even out in the pitch black at night!'

'Why on earth would you want to do that?' Ren asked. 'Wouldn't it just have been easier to catch the bus?'

‘Maybe, but you can’t beat stretching your legs and getting a lung full of fresh air you know, and why go at night? Why to fight the demons of course! Just like Bruce Lee.’

‘I prefer driving,’ Ren muttered.

‘You know what – so do I,’ Said JoJo, ‘or at least I find it easier being driven places, seeing as I can’t drive myself, but I’m afraid that the one doesn’t completely replace the other. I’m certainly hoping to get back to doing some more walking once I’ve recovered from this latest stint in hospital.'

'Good for you,' concluded Ren.

Easy Yoga (do ten of these) :

Lifting the Sky

Yoga is an excellent form of exercise. This is a simple movement a student should try out every day. Ten repetitions, and then rest. At first it may seem boring, or difficult, but with practice and perseverance, the technique should become easy, fluid, and strong.

To describe lifting the sky, start with your hands by your sides, then lift each hand upwards towards the sky until it reaches the peak with both arms outstretched towards the sky. A good way of illustrating this movement is with the analogy of lifting the sun up in the morning, until it reaches its peak at midday, before returning to its resting place at base once more. If you imagine this while practicing the movement, with complete concentration, then you will be doing it right. Easy Tai Chi (do ten of these)

I have drawn a diagram to illustrate this movement, and I hope that you as the reader will take time out to try it at least once, perhaps when you have finished reading today.

JoJo said to Ren : 'I love plays. Have I ever told you how much I love plays?' 'No, go on,' Ren replied.

'Yeah, from Oscar Wilde's The Importance of Being Earnest, to Euripides' The Bacchae, Shakespeare's Macbeth, and Charles Dickens' Oliver Twist. I have had small parts in each of their productions, and I think that they're great plays.

It's the charisma and style that the playwright imbues his work with which facilitates the power in performance. You simply don't get the same impression from the likes of the soaps or much of today's harmless television drama. Oh, and I have also studied Chekhov's The Three Sisters at college which is another powerful play.

Macbeth also is a great piece of poetic and rhythmic narrative. Inspired by the original but not stolen from, I have written some stand-alone soliloquies, to complement the plot about murder, greed, and ambition in the Scottish Highlands all those years ago.

'Earnest' is a romantic comedy, full of intellectual critiques about the politics and high society of the time. And Dickens' Oliver is just a powerful piece of drama I acted in at school as a child and also a local show 'By the Baseball Ground' directed by P, which was a riot. I hope to do some more acting in the future.

Ancient Greek history is one of those great things which nobody knows for sure very much about. All we have left down to us is a collection of mostly incomplete plays and writings telling us about the characters and gods of the time, some epic mausoleums, and legends which have been passed down by word of mouth from that very time.

From these sources, we know that two of the most important gods were Apollo and Dionysus (or Bacchus). One was an athlete/warrior and the other a drunkard and a thespian. Apollo could nail an apple to a fruit tree from a hundred yards, and his brother could drink till the cows came home. Still a god, he was also a lazy nymphomaniac.

Instead of using his Olympic powers to fight the nasty armies or help the poor, he devoted his time to leading women astray and getting drunk.

'So did Apollo kill him then?'

No. Not exactly. No matter how many times the Apollo challenged him, Bacchus would always back down. Then one day, the two died peacefully in their sleep. That being said, the war in their name, between insanity and the sanity, carries on to this day in their name.

Then one day sometime later, JoJo had another revelation. How can history play with the present let alone the future? Surely things that happened before are separate from those which happen now? Maybe so, but if you recognize archetypal figures, then you can accept that people pop up from time to time again throughout history. The hero being the obvious one. Are my heroes the same as the next man's? Probably not.

What about the present. What's a present formula one can apply to famous people to distinguish them from one another? I can only count from personal experience.

11 : Tea

Toby was a young boy who liked drinking cups of tea. This was fortunate because his teacher liked making them. One day, however, unable to resist the temptation of the brew, he crept downstairs early in the morning to make for himself a cup of the fabulous brew. Unfortunately, he made it only as far as the bottom of the stairs before his foot slipped, bringing down with him the tea trolley, cups, saucers, and all. The whole caboodle.

With this his old man stuck his head over the banister and called out :

'Stop thief, I'll have your head for a trophy street-rat!'

Before realizing that it was only his kid, with which he called out again :

'Just get back to bed, I'll clear it up in the morning.'

Which after making a humble apology was exactly what they did.

Luoshi was an old teacher with a penchant for drinking cups of tea. Anyway, one day another of his young students, a fellow called Tan if I remember correctly, ran to him crying.

'Teacher,' he said 'You must help me. It's my wife; she knows not what she does. Either she will raid our piggy bank and spend all our hard-earned pennies, or else she will hoard it all away for a rainy day, but in doing so make me suffer! Please help me, wise one, I have reached my wits end.'

While listening to this, Luo just stroked his grey beard and then, when it was over, raised his hand and said :

'Enough' and 'we will see.'

One week from then, after she had finished bringing in the washing, Mrs. Tan, startled to discover a Ninja dressed in a traditional red and blue kimono pants in the middle of her lawn, sipping a cup of tea. Then on seeing her the Ninja leapt up, bowed down, and held out a clenched fist as if to threaten her.

'If my fist were always like this, what would it be?' He roared. Gaining control of her fear, she ventured, 'Deformed?' 'Correct.' And then he opened his palm and said :

'And if it were always like this, what then?'

'Another kind of deformity,' she said.

'Right again!' he roared. 'If you know that much, then you are a good wife,' he finished before leaping away into the trees. But sure, enough from that day forth Mrs. Tan. helped her husband to spend as well as save.

In the Kunming province of southern China there stands a carving in Chinese which experts in Chinese calligraphy immediately recognize as a masterpiece. Legend has it that it was not carved in a single evening, it actually took old Mr. Foong a long time, or so the story goes...

After his first day at work on the monument, he sat down to admire the fruits of his labor. Then little Ha E Ting (raindrops) appeared with a glass of orange for his pains. He took this and was about to drink it when the boy muttered, 'Rubbish,' before fleeing out of the door. Angered by this insult, old Foong threw down the juice and prepared to give chase before realizing that maybe he had a point and so sat back down to start work refreshed.

A week later the same thing happened again when, after spending a hard day's graft at the marble again, the boy entered with some more juice and again just before leaving the boy told Mr. Foong what he thought of the carving. Again, the old man prepared to chase the rascal, before again hesitating with self-doubt and eventually deciding to start over.

It wasn't until after a year of starting and restarting the work over, did Foong kick the statue over and knowing what the boy was going to say, he had had enough. And just then, again, little Ting appeared with his orange, but this time on seeing the discarded work raised his eyes and said, 'What's this? A masterpiece!' (The word was *'Nor or Lay' love.*)

The pupils of Japanese Zen Buddhism simplify their lives to enrich them. On a nice sunny day three brothers sat down to meditate. Sitting in the shade of an old prune tree, they hoped to discover wonderful things.

The first rule of meditation is silence. This is to give the mind a chance to breathe. Yet a moment had passed, and a tabby cat strolled out into the open in betwixt the three brothers.

They each held their breath as they tried to keep the focus of the exercise on the void. But then the youngest relented and stretched out to stroke the cat. A moment passed and the kid tried to pretend that nothing had happened.

A beat later and the elder one stood up declaring that; 'You've totally ruined my concentration,' and stormed off. Before the middle one whispered, 'idiot,' and the three decided to give up their attempt to meditate altogether!

A Zen student fell upon Jan and said : 'Help me Lord.' 'Whatever is the problem child?' Jan picked up.

'It's my anger. It's dreadful, and when it overtakes me there is nothing which can stand in its way. Whatever can I do?'

'Get a grip on yourself, man,' said the nun before smacking him across the chops. 'Where is your anger now?' she shouted, to which the student had no reply.

The next day the same student returned to the old nun and asked her,

'Oh, help me lady. I'm still angry. It's my mind you see. It chases butterflies, the moon, and even tries to follow rainbows. But the butterflies I can never catch, the moon always seems at arm's length.

out of reach, and the rainbows disappear just before I reach their end. Whatever should I do?'

'Show me,' Jan said.

'What?'

'Show me this anger'

'I cannot,' the student cried.

'Well if you cannot show it to me, then I must conclude that what you are talking about is either a figment of your imagination or else a game you are playing.'

'In the case of the former I suggest a psychologist, and the latter a youth/community worker. Either way, your problem does not concern me so please quit wasting my time.'

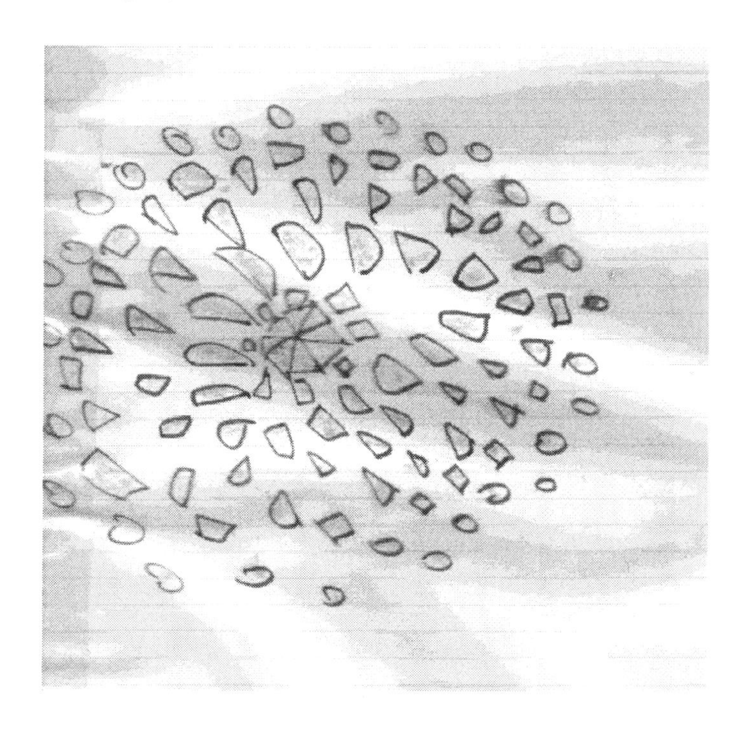

Mr. Chan was a gentleman who liked making and serving cups of tea. Whereas Kong was a fighter who liked killing people. One day Kong thought that he would like to pay a visit to see the other to see what he could do.

So, on the pretext of making a social visit, Kong set out with his sword in its scabbard and despicable intentions in his heart. Then, after being welcomed into the other man's little cottage, the fighter refused to be parted with the weapon when Chan offered to put it in a safe place. Knowing that he was going to have full need of its sharp steel, to swipe the little blighter from the nave to his chops.

Before he quite had the chance to carry out this despicable feat, Kong found himself sat down in a comfy surroundings, listening to quiet pan-pipes playing in the background, and quite hypnotized by the two large red goldfish he noticed swimming around in the tank in the center of the room.

Then he drank his tea, had a little chat, and left, quite forgetting what his evil intentions had ever been in the first place.

12 : Teachers

Mr. Yu was an old teacher who was much loved by his friends and family alike. When he was nearing the end of his years, he called all his students around him and said :

'My children, thank you for staying with me, where others have fled. I fear my time on this Earth is ending. I have helped to teach you, and you have helped me. But now I need you to help me for one last time. Tell me which one of you is going to pick up my robe and medicine bowl and continue from where I leave off?'

Nobody answered.

'Tell Me!' he boomed.

As he did so Master Chan stepped forward. Curiously , Yu observed as the boy reached out and pushed his bowl forward a little way, but curiosity turned to rage when Chan looked up with pleading eyes as if to suggest that this small gesture could somehow commend a scholarship.

'Get out of my sight!' he yelled.

So, the boy reached out and put the bowl back.

a pause

Followed by a smile breaking out across the old man's features.

'You little rascal,' he said. 'For all this time and you've got to see my whole body. Take the bowl and cloak,' he finished, 'they're yours.'

Mr. Guan was a monk. As a youth, he burned his sacred books and instead let the tide of life take him wherever it may. Now, he was getting old and decided to call his students around him for one last time.

'Children' he said. Today I want you to take up my robe and bowl as abbot of this monastery, but which one of you will it be?'

No one stepped forward. Then little Abigail who had always been so quiet, did.

'Oh, great sir,' she said. 'Let us separate to go our different ways. I want to climb hills and watch the little people scurrying around like ants below them; my brothers may want to do other things. Now let us part but always be united!' And with this a cheer erupted from amongst the monks in the hall and an old smile broke across Guan's leathery face.

Then little Yeong stood up and began, 'Ladies and Gentlemen, Mesdames et Messieurs, I hope to live in the cities but not be overwhelmed by them, rather to resist and reform them at the same time. I want to live with others and without them. In them and outside them – can you understand me? No!?'

With which he sat down with a rather disgruntled look on his face.

Then it was Crying Tiger the Indian boy's turn to speak and he said :

'Can I start another school in this old place, and maybe invite some new faces as well?'

At which point old Guan threw down his hat and boomed :

'Never, never in a million years will I let you do this. Turn this old monastery into one of them new-fangled youth clubs, bringing in all the dirt and disease that the monks of this school have worked so hard to eradicate over the years. Be gone now you impostor, and I never want to see your puny face again.'

So, he was evicted for just suggesting a change.

Mr. Luo had been our family's teacher for seven generations. His was the smiling face to present the children with their first pencil and rulers, and the last to shake their hands before graduation out into the big wide world.

Now was Master Lee's turn. He was the youngest of our family and was grateful to receive the certificate. After Luo had passed him the heirloom, he was horrified to see the boy thrust it into the fire, because he saw no need for that old book!

Mr. Luo was also the abbot of a little monastery in the southern Chinese city of Canton (formerly Guangzhou). He required his students to work hard and play hard too. Miss Feng was a little woman from China who fancied herself as something of a Zen protégé. She decided to enroll at the school.

On meeting her, Mr. Luo shook his head and said :

'No that will never do.' Referring to her alluring good looks as a sure sign to disrupt his otherwise exclusively male brotherhood of monks. The lass insisted and was always eventually allowed in on the condition that she wear a veil. This she grudgingly agreed to do, and so the first female monk joined the monastery.

However, despite the veil, the abbot still noticed quite a stir she caused in the brotherhood. Like the ripples in a pond when you throw in a large stone. Then when his wife told him some malicious rumors about the poor girl (such that she was unclean etc.) Luo decided that he had had enough. With this he went to Miss Feng and explained to her that even if it be through no fault of her own, she had to go.

Miss Feng was devastated and in a fit of rage later that evening, she took a lit torch, and burnt the old temple to the ground. For this she was duly arrested and incarcerated. Thus, being forced to spend another eight years of her life facing the same dull matt grey walls of a prison cell.

But for what it's worth, whilst inside she did find another like-minded individual with whom she was able to have evening chats with and find some solace in what must have been otherwise an intolerable situation.

Barry was a hard worker. He would work besides his children even into the ripe old age of seventy. One day some of his children decided that he was overdoing it and hid away his watering can, so he could work no more.

On discovering this, Mr. Barry sat down and refused to get up again for his breakfast. The same thing happened for lunch and by tea-time most of the students were getting desperate. Then, when the two bright sparks whose good idea it had been to hide the can, had the even better one of putting it back : the good sir just smiled and got back to business, muttering to himself, 'No work, no play.'

Gaytan was a strict monk. He taught his pupils discipline and expected obedience in return. Every afternoon he would ask one of his children to ring the bell to announce lunch. One day, when it was the new boy Max's turn to ring the bell, he hesitated. Gaytan noticing that the gong was late, stepped out from behind the bushes dressed in a regal ceremonial Samurai costume with a Shinobi Katana raised high above his head.

Just as he was about to cut the boy, Max hit the bell with such force that Gaytan dropped the sword and hiccupped in annoyance. Then the students tucked into the tastiest and greatest meal they had ever eaten. And all old Gaytan was able to do, was polish his boots and go back to chasing butterflies.

Mr. XiaoGong was a good teacher, yet when his cat died something died inside him also. He finished teaching, packed up his bags and left, never to be seen again. Master Song had been one of XiaoGong's best students and he especially missed his tutor's words of wisdom.

One day some years later a visit to another friend on the outskirts of town, Song noticed a little tramp by the side of the road. Without hesitation he reached over into his pocket for some small change to give to the beggar, when he noticed the unmistakable eagle-shaped birthmark above the elder's right eye.

Straightaway he realized that he had found his old teacher. Try as he might, Xiao Gong could not for the faintest remember who he was. The years had clearly paid their toll on him.

Nevertheless, Song vowed to bring him back to the civilized community. Yet Xiao Gong wouldn't budge. He said :

'It is better to lead a life without material possessions, than to have them and not live at all.' Unable to leave his old friend once more, master Song sat down with the man to investigate what he meant by living without possessions.

So, they bathed in cold water, ate cold food, drank from the stream, and slept under the moon. Sometime later after this had been going on, they came across the shriveled bones of another wanderer lying at the side of the road, starved from the lack of a sustenance diet.

Xiao Gong immediately pounced upon the withered flesh and gnawed the meat from the bones of it as if it was his last meal. Song was unable to touch the dead man's food.

In Tokyo in twelfth Century BC there lived two teachers with completely different ways of teaching. The first was a little man called Hey. Hey was unimposing and really no trouble at all. The second was a large man called Hong. In contrast to Hey, Hong was sometimes aggressive and always overbearing. Some of his students couldn't stand him on account of this. Both teachers had a loyal following and were completely unaware of the other's presence. Until one day on the way to market, they met.

Hong laughed out loud and held out a beer can offering Hey a drink. Hey politely refused saying :

'Thanks, but no, I won't touch the stuff.'

With this Hong frowned muttering, 'If you don't drink, you can't be human!' To which Hey frowned and said, 'So what am I then?' Before they parted never to meet again.

Mr. Mumbai was the abbot of a small monastery in northern China. Yet whereas the other temples would hold noisy celebrations and loud and debauched feasts, Mr. Mumbai liked peace and quiet, and asked his pupils to do the same. So instead of noisy parties they had quiet congregation, and instead of rude awakenings they had peaceful prayer. One day the neighbors heard the church bells ringing, and then they knew that the old man had died.

When JoJo was a boy, his teacher asked him to find the sound of one hand clapping. But try as he might, he couldn't hear anything. So finally admitting defeat the boy went to him and asked for help.

'What?' grunted the teacher, 'Be gone with you.'

On which JoJo, toppled over and lay dead still on the floor. The teacher walked over to him and prodded him with his stick.

'Ow!' JoJo said. 'Dead men can't speak,' the teacher finished. 'Get out!'

One day when Thomas was giving a lecture on the power of love, an intruder burst into the parlor where he was speaking, waving a red banner, and chanting.

'What is the meaning of this?' Thomas asked.

'My God can feed the world and still have food left over for dessert! Can yours do that?' He screamed.

Thomas thought before saying :

'I'm not sure. He feeds me when I'm hungry and rests me when I'm tired. You know what – I think our two gods must be friends.'

'Get out!' Tom finished.

Mr. Lu was a stout man with a big heart. He never wanted to be rich or famous. Leave that for royalty and celebrities. All he wanted was to be happy. Whenever Mr. Lu met a rich man, he would smile, bow his head, and ask for a little change, then was on his way. He always used it to buy sweets and toys for the children, and this way came to be known as the Happy-China- Man.

The man asked Ren Yuecheng,

'Why did our enlightened hero leave India?'

The monk replied :

'An oak tree grows strong over time, but that can't last forever.'

He then asked : 'Is there a teaching that no man has ever taught?' Yuecheng said there was.

A farmer once approached the old monk, Mr. Ibrahim Khan, in need of advice.

'Please help me sir?' he asked. 'My wife has recently died, and I feel troubled.' 'Allah Ta-Ala Wa Salam,' the monk quietly sang.

(Which is roughly translated as God is Great). As he did, a sense of calm filled the air. When he had finished the man looked up, and asked, 'Were you praying for her?'

'I was,' said the monk. With Muslim inspiration.

Yu visited a small monastery in Tibet to get away from the hubbub of everyday life. Up there in the mountains he was cooked nice food, and had a good chance to reflect upon the ceiling of the world. Then a week later, at the end of his pilgrimage, he returned a new man.

Sally asked her teacher to show her the way, but her teacher just gave her a book of maps and told her to find it herself!

My old teacher once told me that the road to enlightenment is like a high mountain path strewn with ice and rocky crevasses on each side. Dare we step forward?

Master Yu's teacher was an old man who used to take regular afternoon siestas, but he forbade his pupils from doing any such thing. Instead, he demanded that they work right the way through the summer heat. On one fine Monday afternoon, however, he caught little Yao doing just that. Before he had time to catch his breath and nab the little blighter, the boy stood up and cried out :

'Please sir, no sir, I was only trying to meet the saints of old'.

'Did you meet them – what did they say?' the teacher hesitated.

'I saw one, but he told me to go back to sleep!' Yao announced, before legging it.

13 : Food

Mr. Kenji the Traveler

There was once a traveler, Mr. Kenji, who liked eating. Everywhere he went to he ate some of the local cuisine. Hence in India he had Mushroom Bhuna, with Pilau Rice and Naan Bread, in China he ate Cantonese Spring Rolls with Egg Fu Yung and Vegetable Chow Mein, in Britain Fish and Chips and Cheese and Tomato Toasties, out in the Wild West he ate beans and steaks.

One day when out walking the hilly ranges of Somerset, he came across a house where all they did was eat rice and more. He thought this was quite unusual until he sat down and tried some for himself. Then he tasted and ate some of the nicest whole meal rice you ever have eaten, so nice in fact that he immediately broke out into song in thanks for the owners. It was, you see, unusually good food.

'Are you hungry?' JoJo asked Ren. 'I know I certainly am. I'd now like to show you how to cook nice rock cakes.'

107

This was when they were both released from prison, and so JoJo had access to an electric stove at his new flat. First thing : wash your hands. Next sieve into a large plastic bowl a mug-full of flour. I prefer to use wholegrain, but it's just a question of personal preference. Then add the other ingredients : a 45-gram slab of butter, a handful of desiccated coconut, another of sultanas and a spoonful of milk.

Then you must use your fingers to rub the butter into the flour, all the whilst mixing well all the other ingredients. At first you should find the milk congealed to some parts of the mixture leaving other parts dry and dusty. When you reach the halfway stage, the mixture should appear more thoroughly wet through, if still of a somewhat uneven ragged texture. Then knead the mixture into a flat base at the bottom of the bowl. This regulates the dough and makes it all even.

Lastly, you should crumble all the dough in-between your fingers trying to reach that famed bread-crumb like texture you often hear the pros talk about. Because the dough is so well mixed in at this stage, you may find yourself feeling pained now, but persevere. The more effort you spend now crumbling it up now, the better it will rise in the oven.

Next, cook for about twenty to twenty-five minutes at a good 180° or until it starts to smell good, then take it out of the oven and leave it to cool for another half an hour. You should be left with a tasty and nutritious pudding/snack.

Mr. Way was a little man with a big appetite. Every Sunday he would arrive home after a hard day's graft at the office and expect to find on the table a fresh plate of steaming beef and mutton stew (his favorite), prepared for him by his loving wife only a short time before.

On some days however, bored of the meat, she would declare herself an organic vegetarian and instead serve up green salad and carrots. This wasn't what Way liked at all. When she did, he would erupt in such a rage that hell hath no greater fury, and thus spoiling an otherwise nice domestic occasion.

It was not long before the emperor himself heard of this problem and dispatched one of his best men to sort it out. So sure enough when on the next Sunday afternoon Way came home expecting meat but not finding it, no sooner had he raised his temper and characteristically blew his lid, as from behind the silk curtain stepped not his wife but a regal Samurai ready to strike.

The warrior was quick to react and drew his sword high above his head before bringing it down to an inch of Way's cheek, stopping just short of some serious damage. Mr. Way never argued with his spouse again after that.

Lu Se Cha was a monk with a big appetite and a short memory. Frequently, he forgot how much he had eaten and so ate some more just to make sure. He was lazy, but that didn't matter because he had a good heart.

Anyway, one day when travelling between cities, carrying a large bundle of cotton, Lu Se Cha lay down to rest beneath two old bamboo trees. He fell asleep and had a nice dream.

Upon awakening, he was horrified to discover that the bundle of cotton that he had been carrying on his journey was gone, and so he hastily rushed to the local magistrate's court to see if the country's justice systems could solve the problem.

The police were promptly on his case, but despite searching high and low all they could find was a little stone Buddha sitting in place where the cloth was before. So, by a process of elimination they deducted that it must be the culprit.

Buddha was duly charged, and failing to enter a plea despite intensive questioning, was locked up for the maximum sentence permitted to the judge, twenty-five years in the slammer. He didn't seem to care, however. He was you see, made of stone.

There once a happy monk called Jason, who was fat because he ate lots of pies. He was also happy because he ate lots of ice-cream too. He was also kind, and although he didn't realize it, people loved him because of this.

One of the kind things he did was to take presents into the park and feed the pigeons. Now although they couldn't thank him in human words, they did flap their wings with that little bit of extra grace, when flying away from him as if to say, 'thank you', like only a pigeon knows how.

Something else which they did is cooed more so that the children laughed whenever they heard them. In this way they cheered up their parents who always liked to hear the children laugh. So, although indirectly, Jason became known as the laughing monk. Yet all he did was feed the pigeons.

Jackson was a gambler. Every day he went to work and every evening he visited his local casino, the Felix Royale. Then every time, bewildered by the flashing lights and scantily dressed ladies, he plunged straight for the slot machines either too afraid or too clever to flutter his cash away on the bigger roulette wheels or any of the other more hard-core tables, reserved for those with an even bigger problem than himself.

Sure, as clockwork, he would lose five, ten or fifteen pounds at a time on one of the one-armed bandits. Knowing when his luck had run out, he would cut his losses and leave just those few pounds down every night.

Until one evening he had the guts, charmed by a recent twenty-five-pound win on a damned slot machine, to move up in the world to the black-jack table. But Jackson was no fool, and so rather than flutter his cash away on a lousy eight or seven he would wait until the royalty showed their faces before showing the colour of his money. So, when that queen of diamond the Ace showed her beautiful face, then still the more he knew his luck and came in.

Did he bet, boy did he bet?! And a second regal accompaniment to his prodigy meant his luck had come in. Even though the house holds the banker's advantage, Jackson's strategy worked. He gambled and played, until one day he won a hundred pounds which he considered, quite rightly, to be a stroke of very good luck.

A long time ago in a faraway land, a lone red fox prowled the hills looking for something to eat. Down in the village, young Alex was talking to an old man.

'Father,' he asked him, 'Why do you endlessly gaze into the clouds noon or night? Isn't there something better for you to do?'

'Er,' the bloke said, and 'leave me alone.' Then : 'Listen our kid, many years ago I too was a young lad like yourself. I thought I had everything : money, looks, the whole caboodle. But now I have nothing. I have squandered it away and for what, a few laughs? Bah. Still my dreams are young if my body is old and getting older by the minute.'

'Is there nothing I can do for you?' asked little Alex. 'Not likely,' said the old chap. 'I had my chance and blew it.' But after that day the fox on the hill was nowhere to be found.

14 : More Stories

Little Benjamin once approached a great king and gave him a little pebble thinking it to be some precious jewel. The king thanked him and pretended that it was. But later, Benjamin was himself reborn as a great king.

One day when out amongst the fields, Jane came across a rich looking gentleman and asked him for 50p.

'Begone with you,' he snarled. 'What do you take me for?'

'Sorry boss, I was just trying to get something to eat,' she relented.

There once was a group of barbarians who went from village to village destroying everything in their path. People were terrified of them until one day a young stranger with a foreign accent stepped out and said :

'Which one of you men will join me to fight these villains?'

After this a group of the settlement's bravest and strongest young men gathered around him. Then suddenly, the barbarians were heard from the adjoining hills and terrified, some of the hero's followers began to step back. Noticing their panic, he yelled :

'Do not fear lads, look I will ask the gods to

decide. Heads up we win!'

He then threw a copper coin high into the air caught it and declared heads before leading his small group into and through the helpless enemy. Later that day when cleaning up, a young street urchin noticed a small coin lying at the side of the road. He couldn't discern whether it was heads or tails, but picked it up and pocketed it, nevertheless.

Once upon a time there lived three hedgehogs: a big one, a little one, and a medium one. They came up to a busy road and the little one walked across without any trouble. Then the medium sized one did the same, crawling beneath the middle of the cars. But when the big one's turn came about, he hesitated as if he could feel something was wrong. Then he just turned around and walked away. And why?

Because you see that was when an old Robin Reliant (three-wheeler) had driven up and over the highway, and so by retreating the big hedgehog saved his own life. By saying no when the others had said yes had escaped that rare but indomitable middle wheel, which would have squashed him had he crossed at the above-mentioned time.

So, the moral of the story is doesn't follow hedgehogs? Nah man, hedgehogs are cool. The moral is I say, don't cross the road without first looking both ways.

There was once an old university professor called James. James knew a lot; he had a post graduate degree in something or another and had worked in several prestigious institutions across the country. He still felt, however, that something was missing from his life, and was prepared to travel the world in search of this unknown quandary.

One day he heard of a wise old man who lived on a distant shore, whose knowledge was such that it surpassed all others'. Hence, he set out, travelling for many days and nights until he reached the doorstep of this clever person.

He knocked on the door and was shown into a warm comfortable room. After shaking hands, they both sat down and began to chat about the weather. Then James's host asked him :

'Have you had a safe and pleasant journey?'

'I did indeed,' the professor replied. 'How has your day been?'

'Oh fine, fine,' said the proprietor. 'Here, how rude of me, you must be thirsty, let me get you a cup of tea?'

Which James accepted as he was feeling a bit parched after his travels. However no sooner than the man had started pouring the brew, did James notice a mischievous glint in his eye, and not a moment later, but the old man overfilled the cup and poured tea all down the good doctor's trousers.

'Stop!' he cried in astonishment. 'This is exactly what you must do.' The host replied. 'You already know enough,' Before showing him the door.

Once upon a time in a little village in China there lived a kind lady called Judy. She had long supported a monk on the hill by bringing him hand-knitted jumpers to wear and freshly cut sandwiches to eat. And so, things seemed happy for a while.

Then on one wet and windy morning, Judy awoke to hear a little tapping at her door. On opening it she found a terribly upset girl in a beautiful if wet special dress. The girl was crying. Judy kindly offered, 'Whatever is the matter, love?'

To which Lucy replied between sobs, 'Unhung, I have been spurned by my loved one,' and 'Ung, she cheated on me when we were due to marry, boo-hoo!' With this Judy took the distraught girl into her arms and brought her into the house. She said, 'There, there, please don't cry – listen I know a monk who lives over there on the hill, do you see? I think he has got something for you.'

So, when it had stopped raining, Miss Lucy set off to find out what exactly it was she had waiting for her. An hour passed by, whereupon Judy thought that everything had settled down once again. However quite soon again she heard the familiar tip-tip-tap on her door and on opening it was dismayed to find the girl standing before her again, crying once again.

She said, 'He just told me that 'an old tree grows firm on the chilly mountain rock, nowhere is there any warmth,' before kicking me out!'... That night Judy burnt the monk's house down.

Little Miss Feng lived in a city in the far south (Vietnam) and was renowned across the land for the incense burners she made. One day, the mayor of the city approached her and asked if she could make him one. She said she would be honored to and got to it right away.

Miss Feng also used to hold long and debauched parties where a whole host of guests would get up to a range of nasty and unspeakable things, which for that time in Vietnam was unheard of. So that by the time the mayor returned to collect his gift it was not ready. The young woman got down on her knees and apologized to him profusely and insisted it would be ready shortly. But as the days turned to months and the months into years, still the mayor waited.

Then one day, tired of waiting, he paid a surprise visit to Miss Feng (to see what was taking her so long). Through the window he carefully watched as she painted the pipe with elaborate designs and detail. But then he was horrified to observe her hold the much sought after gift high above her head and in a flash throw it down to the floor where it smashed into a million smithereens, having decided that yet again the present fell short of the beautiful perfection which she had sought. The mayor left empty handed and thoroughly displeased.

King was an ordinary man with an extra-ordinary heart. One day he had the good fortune to win the national lottery. Rather than waste it on himself or put it in the bank to rot, he decided to buy presents for the children and jewelry for his friends. Because of this everybody was happy, and everybody loved him.

Sometime after that he discovered a young woman standing on a riverbank trapped, with flood waters gushing all around. This was whilst out walking the dog. King however wasn't fazed and tying the dog to a tree carried the maiden across the river to safety. For this act of heroism, she was eternally grateful, and they got married soon after. But it was not long after that when King came home to discover a dreadful racket going on upstairs in the room above him of the honeymoon apartment.

Afraid that he had been surprised by some impostor, he grabbed the nearest hard thing (a fire poker) and ran to save her. As he got up to the door it dawned on him that despite her being with a stranger, he wasn't exactly unwelcome. With that King realized he could never make his angel happy, so he left never to see her again.

Mr. Yao was a hardworking man much loved by his family and friends. One day he received a letter from his sisters foreboding some bad tidings. They said that their son, his nephew, was wasting far too much money on some girl and pleaded with their brother to come home and salvage matters before it was too late.

Yao knew for himself the power some women could hold over certain men, because he had himself fallen foul of them on more than one occasion, apparently. So, he agreed to return and dutifully see what could be done.

On arriving at the door, he was greeted by a young man who warmly embraced him before making him a nice, hot cup of tea. He then knew he had found the right place. The two began to talk about things, nothing you understand, they just chatted and had a nice day sitting in the garden.

Then the young nephew brought out his guitar and together they sang and played songs. Silver also showed the boy how to do bar chords which is a technique where you fix the index of your left hand to slide it up and down the fretboard in a fixed position. All the while strumming or plucking with the right and in case you don't have the foggiest idea about what I just said, don't sweat it. This method is best taught by a good teacher.

It was not until late into the evening did old Yao pack up his bags and set off again on the long journey home, and not once did he mention the young lady. He didn't have to.

King was a kind man much loved for his warmth and compassion. Mary was a little village girl who one day came across a child in her pram. Immediately, she pointed her finger at King who the whole village set upon, as if he was the most evil man in the entire world.

Yet throughout the child's upbringing not once did he miss a payment. Until at last many years later, on her child's birthday did Miss Mary relent and confess that the real father was a local statesman.

But still Mr. King kept his promise and was a good father to the child which knew him. Thus, it grew up into a strong young adult loving both of its very real parents who gave it the chance to start life in the world without them.

15 : Poetry

We live in a world of poems and poets with their tongues cut. Music and melodies. Life's like a chess game black versus white, but who's right? Not if you're on the other side of the board and where does Buddha sit? With the winner, the loser, the board itself? How about with the football I think that's more likely? But I'm no footballer So, my glimpse of Buddha must be his thoughtful side. Like in the games when I win Or when I win the games I lose.

I mean when both sides struggle, and the outcome means something.

Learning French is a lot like playing chess. I only understand a fragment of it, but what I do understand is immensely rewarding. So where does smoking fit into this equation? Probably as the Nemesis. The uncontrollable power of defeat Grasps at me and pulls me into its irresistible murky depths and how do I fight it? Ten pushups? Yes sir.

On one nice morning two kids got talking 'Where are you going?' the first said to one. 'I am following the voice of bird-song' the other replied. On the next day much the same 'Where are you going?'

'I'm following the lane' she cried.

On day three again it was 'Where today?'

'I'm going to play, will you come with me?'

'I'll come with you' he cried.

What does it feel like to be lost in the whirlpool of life and stumbling? Down and down and around with no-where to go. No-where left to run trapped like a pig in a hole, or a parrot in a tree out of moves, out of air, out of life.

Desperate always looking for an answer to a riddle. Which seems unsolvable or the chord to a riff which seems unplayable. Desperate, hopeless, angry, frustrated, or just confused. But not bitter and not anxious, just a little bit sad and afraid.

Sometimes worried about the past and the future but now working on today.

16 : Even More Stories

Mary was an old monk who was also the abbot of an old monastery up in the hills. One day she gathered her students around her and waited until they were quiet before speaking.

'Everyone listen,' she said. 'My time on this land is ending.' A hush filled the room.

'Now I want to choose one of you to succeed me as my successor. So, I have devised a question and he, or she, who can answer it, will get the job.'

All eyes were on the glass of water which she revealed from behind her back.

'My question to you is this. Is this glass half full or half empty?'

The students were stumped, and realizing the importance of the task set them, none wanted to risk the humiliation of making the wrong answer. That was until Gaitan the cook stepped forward, drank the water said, 'half full' and left by the nearest exit. But without realizing how close he had stepped to the mark, Gaitan was overjoyed to hear the next day that the abbot had reconsidered her decision and decided that the job was his.

Mrs. Ye was on her last bed. She had lived a good life and was quite sorry to have reached the end of it. Mr. Xing Che, one of her good friends, went to her and touched her.

'My dear' he said, 'can I help you?'

'I fear,' she smiled, 'it is too late for any of that.'

He laughed as they held hands and she died. But he kept his word.

In the days of the venerable Yue Fei a great outdoor feast was to be held celebrating the marvel and miracles of the world. Princes and princesses from all over were invited to take part in the celebrations, and they all came.

Foong was a little man with a big heart, and whilst he hadn't exactly received an invitation himself as such, he had heard about the event and decided it was just too important to miss. So, saddling up his horse, he set out on the long journey there. But unfortunately for him he had got his dates mixed up and arrived to see the last of the other guests leaving.

All that remained was a little girl sitting in the middle of a tent in what appeared to be a deep sleep. On closer inspection however he realized that she was in fact in trance and was indeed aware of his every move. So Foong asked her,

'My friend, I have spent a long time thinking about the riddle and I understand that its solution requires a greater effort than any one man or woman can claim in their own lifetime. But so then why is it that I am still looking for the last piece of the great jigsaw of life?'

The girl just smiled and said :

'The gateless gate is wide open. All you have to do is step through it.'

Then she disappeared, and he did too.

Grant was an old man. He was quite content but one day decided that he wanted to go on a journey to try and find the end of the rainbow. On the morning he was about to leave, his old friend Joey stopped him.

'Where are you going?' Joey asked.

'I'm not sure,' was the reply. 'Can I come with you?' Joey asked again.

Now he hesitated; Grant knew that his time was ending, and he had to make the journey on his own. But he hadn't forgotten the friendship Joey had shown him over the years. So, he ultimately thought that it was the least he could do, and the two agreed to set off together in search of the place where the sun never sets.

Judy was a kind woman. When she had reached the end of her years, she lay down to rest. Then her little student, Min crept up behind her and whispered, 'Guess who?'

'Quit messing about,' Judy scolded, 'can't you see I'm dying?'

'Oh, I'm sorry,' the girl replied sheepishly. Before whispering, 'What does it feel like, to die I mean?'

'It feels like nothing you can ever imagine,' Judy spoke.

'But what does that feel like?' Min insisted. With which Judy just closed her eyes and tried to imagine the unimaginable. She thought about the sound water makes when it falls off rocks from a great height, and she thought about the rays the sun produces when he raises his heavenly sights above the world at the break of dawn. She thought about the gentle breathing of a baby in the middle of the night.

But for all this Judy had neither the inclination nor the energy to begin to try and express her mind to the upstart. So instead she just remarked :

'What's your name child?'

'Min,' the girl muttered.

'Have you ever heard the sound of one hand clapping Min?

'Umm,' she mused, 'I don't think so.'

'Or thought about what your kid's name will be?'

'But I don't have any children,' Min answered. With which Judy closed her eyes and gently died.

Chi-Hong was a temple buried deep in the heart of the Amazon rainforest which was protected by three stone edifices that reached high into the sky, (to bar entry from the wandering vagabonds and scoundrels who roam the earth). One day, young Jason set out to investigate what all the fuss was about. Being strong and nimble he climbed over the stone walls without too much trouble but beyond these he found some more imposing barriers.

The first was a great waterfall twenty feet long and a hundred high, which sounded like an entire Amazon battalion beating their war drums and marching into battle. But Jason attacked the rock with the strength of a hero and the courage of a child, so that soon he had climbed atop the mighty beast.

Unfortunately, however, before he quite had the chance to catch his breath, his foot slipped, and he fell. Then the whole of his life flashed before his eyes. So, imagine J's surprise when he next awoke and found himself immersed beneath the deep blue waves and swimming for what seemed like forever. At last he surfaced in an eerie moonlit cavern, where purple water lilies floated on the surface, and the silence was a refreshing balm, from the noise he had just left.

No sooner had he stepped out of the cave and into the depths of the mountain cavern, then he found himself hopelessly and impossibly lost. And so, like a blind sparrow with its wings clipped he blindly and hopelessly stumbled through the dark desperately fumbling from hold to hold. Until just when he had about given up the hope of ever seeing the light of day again, he saw it :

He came out into some lush fields where the bright blue skies and white clouds were above him. Implemented by the shining sun, the lush green fields before him were adorned with Firs and Conifers, Beech and Maple trees.

With BlueTits and the Swallows singing in the air. And the wind rustling through the leaves he sat down. Then the sun gently caressed his tired shoulders and the pigeons cooed their gentle calls. He contemplated happiness.

He decided to quit his lifelong struggle, and just be happy with what he had. So, he never did find that ancient temple hidden in the bowels of the earth. Or did he?

17 : The End

17==21

JoJo braced himself for the final blow. The fight had been going on for far too long, his bones were aching, his blood bleeding from the tiger bites and scratches, and his head aching from the non-stop barrage of abuse and mania which had so far affronted him. He didn't know where he would wake up, and that's if he ever did.

He regretted the crimes he had committed, the sins and misdemeanors. He feared that if our Lord who we face on judgement day is forgiving, the devil is not. And none of us can be sure of which direction we are headed when we finally face those pearly gates.

“Brian! Wake up! It was all a dream. You are not here, you never were. This time you have spent arguing and fighting, stealing, and lying, what was it for? Nothing! Your life is over brother. You have failed the test. The test of our brothers and sisters, elders, and street men.

And as you lie there on the pavement, and your final tears shed down your face, give a moment to me. Think about the homeless man you ignored for all these years. The comedian, who was funny, the thief who got caught, and now faces the same walls, the same baked potatoes, the same curled smoke day in on day, for the rest of his years.

And think of this, you may not be that person, maybe you never were. But the things you have said and done, will be remembered, if not by you then by your heavenly father, and so when, one day you do face me, up above, remember, that I am here, I always was. And whilst this life is not always the easiest road, it is what it is, nonetheless.

I love you. I AM LOVE. I am all the parents and lovers, the bredrin and sisters and mothers. With me you can go a long way. And without me, you are stranded alone and sluggish. We can make it together, so remember my name. My name is He that is and has always been. The chance for freedom at the end of the sentence, the hope at the end of the tunnel, the gold at the bottom of the rainbow. And the light from the sun,

I don't know what your name is. It doesn't matter. You could be reading this in India Japan, or the Commonwealth. What us important is that you are engaging, learning building, and taking on from where I leave off. I won't always be here. I fear my best days are ending, just as yours are just beginning. Please trust in the Lord and his Wife mother nature, for theirs was the Kingdom, power, and the glory, and when you run out of options, turn to them, and let us all pray that they provide

References

ASSORTED. (1914) The Holy Bible Douay Version New York : John Murphy Company

BAUDELAIRE. (1964) Les Fleurs du Mal & Autres Poémes. Paris : Garnier-Flammarion

CARR, A. (1987) The Easy Way to Stop Smoking London : Penguin Books

CONZE, E. (1969) Buddhist Scriptures. London : Penguin Classics

DIAMOND, H. & DIAMOND, M. (1985) Fit for Life. London : Bantam books

DOGEN. trans. NISHIJIMA, W. and CROSS G. (1994) Shobogenzo London : Windbell publications

EVOLA, J. (1998) Meditations on the Peaks. Vermont : Inner Traditions International

FRAGER, R. and FADIMAN, J. (2000) Essential Sufism. San Francisco : Harper Collins

HERZOG, M. (1997) Annapurna : The first conquest of an 8000 metre peak. London : Pimlico

HUGO, V. (1994) Les Misérables. Hertfordshire : Wordsworth Editions Limited

HUMPHREYS, C. (1953) Concentration and Meditation; A Manual of Mind Development . London : Watkins

KIT, W. K. (1996) The Art of Shaolin Kung Fu. London : Element Books

MASCARÓ, J. (1962) The Bhagavad Gita. London : Penguin Classics

NYE, R. Trans. (1995) Beowulf. London : Orion

REPS, P. & SENZARKI, N. Trans. (1957) Zen Flesh Zen Bones. Juliana : Penguin Books

SHAKESPEARE, W . (2007) Macbeth. London : Penguin Popular Classics

TERRELL, P . (2005) Langenscheidt Pocket Chinese Dictionary. Berlin and Munich : Langenscheidt KG

TZE, L. ADDIS, S. & LOMBARDO, S. Trans. (1993) Tao Te Ching. Indiana : Hackett Publishing Company